Samuel French Acting Edition

The End of the Line
Beauty Meets the Beast

by Tom Chiodo

SAMUEL FRENCH

FOR PRODUCTION INQUIRIES

UNITED STATES AND CANADA
info@concordtheatricals.com
1-866-979-0447

UNITED KINGDOM AND EUROPE
licensing@concordtheatricals.co.uk
020-7054-7200

Each title is subject to availability from Concord Theatricals Corp., depending upon country of performance. Please be aware that *THE END OF THE LINE – BEAUTY MEETS THE BEAST* may not be licensed by Concord Theatricals Corp. in your territory. Professional and amateur producers should contact the nearest Concord Theatricals Corp. office or licensing partner to verify availability.

No one shall make any changes in this title(s) for the purpose of production. No part of this book may be reproduced, stored in a retrieval system, scanned, uploaded, or transmitted in any form, by any means, now known or yet to be invented, including mechanical, electronic, digital, photocopying, recording, videotaping, or otherwise, without the prior written permission of the publisher. No one shall share this title(s), or any part of this title(s), through any social media or file hosting websites.

For all inquiries regarding motion picture, television, online/digital and other media rights, please contact Concord Theatricals Corp.

MUSIC AND THIRD PARTY MATERIALS USE NOTE

Licensees are solely responsible for obtaining formal written permission from copyright owners to use copyrighted music and/or other copyrighted third-party materials (e.g., artworks, logos) in the performance of this play and are strongly cautioned to do so. If no such permission is obtained by the licensee, then the licensee must use only original music and materials that the licensee owns and controls. Licensees are solely responsible and liable for clearances of all third-party copyrighted materials, including without limitation music, and shall indemnify the copyright owners of the play(s) and their licensing agent, Concord Theatricals Corp., against any costs, expenses, losses and liabilities arising from the use of such copyrighted third-party materials by licensees. For music, please contact the appropriate music licensing authority in your territory for the rights to any incidental music.

IMPORTANT BILLING AND CREDIT REQUIREMENTS

If you have obtained performance rights to this title, please refer to your licensing agreement for important billing and credit requirements.

For Annie

THE END OF THE LINE – BEAUTY MEETS THE BEAST was first performed at the Sagamore Resort in Lake George, New York in October, 1988. The production was produced by Murder A la Carte and directed by Tom Chiodo. The cast was:

DOCTOR HEINRICH VON SCHTOOPTENSTEIN ....Robert Zukerman
COQUETTE VON SCHTOOPTENSTEIN MULLER ....Kay Towne
ANNABELLE .... Rosemarie Himes
LOUIE..Larry Reed
FRANCES ....Casey Wayne
VICTOR ....Michael Dane
ARNOLD ARMSTRONG...........................Tony Hamill
CASWELL HUDDLESTONE....................George Himes

PIANIST...James Followell

Note: The role of Arnold Armstrong may be played by a man or woman—Arnold or Ann Armstrong.

The script can be performed as a one-evening or weekend event. All scenes are performed for both types of productions.

CHARACTERS

Doctor Heinrich Von Schtooptenstein: Bizarre, ardent, confused, comical mad-scientist type. Speaks with heavy German accent. Infamous founder of the private foundation, THE SOCIETY FOR THE ADVANCEMENT OF BEAUTY THROUGH TISSUE RESEARCH. [pronounced tis - sue] He has an M.D. in biomedical research, a Ph.D. in abnormal psychology, and a doctorate in veterinary medicine. He wears, at all times, a white lab coat, medical ID tag "Dr. Von Schtooptenstein," stethoscope, and rubber gloves. Facial tissues are stuffed in all of his pockets. His gray hair is always in disarray and he displays behavioral tics. He frequently uses scientific terminology with slips of the tongue (i.e. referring to guests as specimens, victims, guinea pigs, etc.). Age: fifty. Costume on Saturday morning is same as above except that shirt and pants are replaced with pajamas.

Coquette Von Schtooptenstein Muller: Coquette (Beauty) was the once married, now divorced, twenty-four year old estranged daughter of Dr. Von Schtooptenstein. Her brief marriage, set up by her father, is a red herring story for small talk during the event. During the initial part of the event, she may raise suspicion among guests but, generally, is low key and not so obvious an actor. She is not very forthcoming with information about her family history. She does not reveal her maiden name. She resents her father, but because he is family, she will not tell all, with respect to his experimental deeds, even though she was a victim of his experiments. She was not always physically beautiful. She, in her father's mind, is a success story of what his research can accomplish. In her mind, he has ruined her by experimenting and making her physically beautiful. She has siblings, which she doesn't discuss. She does not know that Victor (Beast), with whom she is in love, is her twin brother. She is also, unaware that her mother, who left home when she was very young, is Annabelle (Bag Lady). She displays discreet, animal-like behavior, preening herself, somewhat cat-like in nature. Costume throughout weekend: attractive dresses. She becomes more noticeably well-dressed as the weekend progresses.

ANNABELLE: Annabelle is a bag lady with more clothes on her back than Bloomingdales has on its racks. She carries several bags full of her life's belongings. She, and her sidekick Louie, drunkenly stumble into the convention of Dr. Von Schtooptenstein's foundation. She and Louie wisely spend their welfare checks on listings of conventions, conferences and caucuses where free food, booze and merriment abound. Fortune 500 organizations and five star hotels are their preferences. Louie and Annabelle get along great when they're drunk. When they're not, they often have heated and sometimes physical exchanges. But, they love each other and they understand each other and are content with their situation in life. In fact, they feel that they see life much more clearly from where they stand than does the rest of society. Annie often calls Louie her "favorite Little Shit." They often offer, with satirical style, their political and personal views on significant issues like housing, unemployment, education, etc. Annie often explains that Louie sometimes falls by the wayside when it comes to practicing what she preaches. She decidedly wears the pants in their *household*, which, this weekend, is a cardboard Maytag refrigerator box. Annie has a wild and beautiful laugh. Underneath, there's a lot of hurt. She was Mrs. Heinrich Von Schtooptenstein, before he went mad. She left home twenty-two years ago when the doctor destroyed her family by experimenting on their two children, Coquette and Victor. He turned them into physical beasts. Annie is surprised to see that the gathering that she and Louie are crashing is lead by Heinrich. She is unaware that her two children, Coquette and Victor, whom she hasn't seen in twenty-two years are also present. Age: mid-fifties. One bag lady costume throughout the weekend except for the resolution on Sunday when she appears cleaned-up in a motherly skirt and suit jacket.

LOUIE: Middle-aged, tattered, lovable bag man. Danny DeVito type. Between his and Annabelle's mouth there's not one complete set of teeth. Louie walks with a limp. He claims that it's a wound from WWII. He is devoted to Annie, who calls him "Moonbeam" for his eyes that shine like a full moon on a dark night. He's a good hearted man that has tried all of his life to do right, but somehow he has managed to bungle and botch most of his financial opportunities. Though he tries to overcome it, his weak spot is gambling, the good old "American dream" of instant cash. Louie's old-fashioned values force him to try too hard to improve his and Annie's financial lot. He talks of wild financial endeavors with which he has been involved and engages guests with impractical "get rich quick" schemes. He claims that he is an adviser to the Republican party on fiscal issues and Donald Trump's right-hand bag man. He ends many conversations with his favorite line, "Another day, another dollar, another destiny." One bag man costume throughout weekend.

FRANCES: A drag version of Herman Munster. A flaming red-headed bombshell. She is Heinrich's own "special creation"—a regular mix and match. Her accent is from the Bronx. She has the legs of a Vegas show girl and biceps of a Dallas Cowboy. Heinrich experimented and transformed this creature with spare parts and through tissue regeneration. She has two Frankenstein-type bolts protruding from either side of her neck. She claims to be, on the average, all tolled, twenty-five years old, give or take an appendage. Costume on Friday evening is a brightly colored hospital johnnie. Costume for remainder of weekend is a nurse's uniform, white stockings, white shoes and nurse's cap.

VICTOR: Twenty-five-year-old son of Heinrich and Annabelle. He does not know that Annabelle is his mother, but he feels a special kinship to her. Over the years, he, too, has fallen in love with Coquette, who has been teaching him slowly to communicate and speak. He does not speak much, mainly because he does not want to communicate with anyone but Coquette, whom the Doctor has kept away from him. He is realistic in appearance as half lion/half man in ragged burlap clothes. Same costume throughout weekend. Though he rarely speaks, he is very intelligent, poetic and eloquent.

ARNOLD/ANN ARMSTRONG (can be played by a man or a woman): An approximately twenty-five to thirty-year-old sharp-tongued, syndicated investigative reporter. S/he is an uninvited and unwanted guest at this event because of his/her ardent pursuit of the infamous Doctor throughout the years. S/he believes that what the Doctor does is illegal and inhuman. S/he has attempted to discredit the Doctor personally and professionally. S/he makes it clear that s/he almost has conclusive proof to substantiate his/her accusations. S/he also mentions occasionally that the Doctor has had experiments that have backfired. Professional conservative dress throughout weekend [man in sport coats and bow ties; woman in pant suits except for Saturday night dress]. S/he carries a camera and shoots pictures of characters, suspects, and guests. Also carries a note pad and interviews guests about the society.

CASWELL HUDDLESTONE: He is a Federal marshal present at this event for purposes of providing undercover government protection. Initially he plays an average fan of Doctor Von Schtooptenstein. When the action requires police attention, he intervenes and keeps the local police out of the melee. A very suspicious character, not above reproach or incrimination, he plays the fed-type—tough and unflappable. He represents the Food and Drug Administration which, under pressure, he reveals is secretly funding part of Doctor Von Schtooptenstein's research. He reveals evidence and information only when he sees fit with the excuse that it is classified information. Since the Doctor's research is being used for a secret government project, not even the local or state police can know about it. He informs the audience that no one leaves the premises and that the Feds will be debriefing each one of them after the murders are solved. Costume: conservative suits throughout weekend.

Note: In this script Armstrong will be referred to as a female character. During weekends, if there is a guest check-in period to work, it is done by Doctor, Coquette, Annabelle, Caswell and briefly by Annie and Louie.

Scene 1

As guests arrive, a sign posted in the entranceway reads:

> *"Welcome Members*
> *To The*
> *Bi-Annual Meeting*
> *of*
> *The Society For the Advancement of Beauty*
> *Through Tissue Research*
>
> *Featured Speaker:*
> *Dr. Heinrich Von Schtooptenstein, Founder."*

A large cardboard box is arranged just outside of the building with a pillow and miscellaneous used items. CHARACTERS make entrances and mingle as guests arrive, in the following order: CASWELL, ARMSTRONG, COQUETTE, DOCTOR. ARMSTRONG interviews guests and characters. CASWELL reacts as a fan of Doctor and breaks the ice for other guests to be interviewed. Each CHARACTER builds anticipation in audience for arrival of the Doctor. COQUETTE reacts shyly then negatively to Reporter. DOCTOR makes a grand entrance and shakes a few hands before the REPORTER snaps a picture of him. The antagonism between Armstrong and Doctor is established immediately during their first interview.

ARMSTRONG. Hold it just like that ... Doctor.
DOCTOR. Oh yes ... Oh you ... You want a picture of the renowned physician?

ARMSTRONG. (*Almost under her breath.*) Quack, quack.

DOCTOR. Click, click? Did you say click? Just shoot Miss Armstrong.

ARMSTRONG. I'd love to.

DOCTOR. You'll be printing this photograph when you are reporting in your puny newspapers my winning the next Nobel prize.

ARMSTRONG. (*With her eye in the camera shooting a picture.*) They don't give trophies to your kind; they give you twenty to life.

DOCTOR. (*Nervously laughs it off.*) Ah hah-hah. (*Passing by her.*) Watch it, I have friends in high places.

ARMSTRONG. The Bronx Zoo?

DOCTOR. If you'll excuse me, I have guests. Ah, look at all of these lovely specimens?

ARMSTRONG. (*Following after him.*) Doctor, why do you always refer to people as specimens.

DOCTOR. I am impervious to your insolence. Go chase after an ambulance Miss Armstrong, my guinea pigs ... er ... I mean ... my guests await me. (*To guests.*) Welcome, welcome to the bi-annual meeting of the National Society for the Advancement of Beauty Through Tissue Research. We're going international next year, you know.

(*HE proceeds to shake hands and mingle with guests. CASWELL walks up to Armstrong, takes her arm discreetly but rather intensely, escorts her away from the Doctor, quietly but sharply asks her who invited her to this event, and suggests that she should refrain from making accusations about the Doctor.*
CHARACTERS continue to work the crowd throughout cocktail period. The DOCTOR distributes organ donor cards to guests to be completed before he begins his

welcome address. The Doctor may assist guests in completing the cards. [Option for Director: for larger audiences, bag people can make a brief appearance during cocktails if additional action is needed in this scene.]
Approximately fifteen minutes before the end of cocktails, the DOCTOR collects and reviews the donor cards then HE steps up to the podium to greet all of the guests. During the delivery of the following, the DOCTOR may gesticulate throughout the speech with the facial tissues stuffed in his pockets; pulling at them; waving them; wiping his forehead; blowing his nose, etc.)

(Musical Intro.)

DOCTOR. (*Pounds gavel.*) May I have your attention please. Thank you. Welcome, welcome, Ladies and germs. (*Musical chord.*) (*Chuckle.*) please excuse the topical humor. My speech writers are on leave of absence.

(Musical tag.)

DOCTOR. I, Doctor Heinrich Von Schtooptenstein, beloved founder, President and Director, officially call to order, the bi-annual meeting of the National Society for the Advancement of Beauty Through Tissue Research. (*Musical underscore for speech.*) In 1955, when Albert Einstein drew his last breath of polluted air, scientists worldwide may have thought that advancement beyond the theory of relativity died with Doctor Einstein. I am here to tell you that there is life beyond time, space and *tissue*!

*(The following can be **read** as a prepared speech with bifocals, however, the more that is memorized, the better the effect.)*

DOCTOR. Yes, for years science has struggled to warp the space-time continuum. For years, science has struggled to create life artificially. To make a dead thing appear to be alive. But, aside from a few feeble attempts with Ronald Reagan ... they have not succeeded.

However, I, Heinrich Von Schtooptenstein, M.D., Ph.D., V.D. am here to reveal to you, that I, *alone* have discovered the secret of the re-animation of dead *tissue*! The essence of life itself! A proverbial fountain of youth! I have succeeded where others have failed! ... Taken the mass of a body in motion as a function of the energy content that varies with velocity, interdependent upon form and four-dimensional continuums, deflecting light rays, warping time and space, not to mention the gravitational fields, and ... when that was all done ... I transformed inanimate, inert, extinct, lifeless *tissue* into living, breathing, vital, organic *tissue*!

Tonight I am ready to reveal to you the results of over twenty-five years of *my* research. Very soon I will reveal it to the world. The name of Von Schtooptenstein will be a household word. Little children will be reading their science books in schools everywhere and they will know that I have done for science what Dan Quayle did for the eighty-eight campaign, to bring youth and vicissitude to lethargic matter. Through mutability, alteration, unpredictable change, variation, shifting circumstance and a few ups and downs, I have created *tissue* that breathes again.

Enough with the paid political announcements. Oh, by the way, before I forget, I would like to thank the Mary Kaye Cosmetics Foundation for their generous contributions and partial sponsorship of this symposium.

Every time you purchase a vial of their wrinkle remover, Mary Kaye donates one dollar to our research. The woman is desperate ... I mean ... determined to help us further the cause of beauty and to eradicate wrinkles from the face of the earth.

On with business. In a little while you're going to see, with your very own eyes, my most secret experiments to date. I hope you are all prepared. Expect the unexpected. Brace yourselves. But now, our first order of business. I would like to officially welcome our new members to the society. *(HE mentions two guests, or on a mystery weekend, he may mention a tour group.)* *(To new members:)* You are very lucky people to be accepted into our secret society. Our membership is *very limited.* It requires a very particular mind set to qualify for admission into the society. You have that mind set. In the words of Ponce de Leon, the Spanish explorer who discovered Florida ... while searching for the Fountain of Youth—our motto: To youth! To Beauty! To Life! To hell with it all! Everyone, I would like all of you, our old members, to join our new members and to repeat the sacred oath of our society.

EVERYONE. To Youth! To Beauty! To Life! To hell with it all!

DOCTOR. It does my cells good to hear that.

Second order of business. I am sure by now that you have all read the rules of the game for our little symposium this weekend. Does everyone agree to the rules of the game on how to conduct yourselves and business from the minute you arrive to the minute you leave? *(HE elicits a "Yes, Doctor.")*

Third order of business. As you know, you are a member of the society because you are either a potential donor or potential candidate recipient of re-animated tissue. As a sort of update and before I reveal my experiments, let us see what all of you have to offer. In other words, let's find out a little about our potential patients. You all filled out a little questionnaire (*For weekends only.*) and a donor candidate card when you arrived. Let us share with our fellow members, the configuration of our group. When I call your name, please raise a limb and indicate that you are alive and present. (*HE then reviews some questionnaires and donor cards for five to seven minutes, calling guests forward and exchanging ad libs with them.*)

(*Looking off toward the dining room.*) Fourth order of business. Dinner is ready. Before you go into the dining room, let me warn you, do not be shocked at what you see. It is a not-so-gentle reminder of why we are here. Don't get too close. It is tame, but you never know. I'll explain more to you when I present my empirical data during dinner. Thank you and carry on.

(*Director's Note: Victor is in place in the dining room before the end of the speech.*)

Scene 2

Entering Dining Room: Guests arrive in the dining room to see VICTOR huddled and chained in a corner. A straw area is made for him to rest. A bowl of water is also in the corner. The DOCTOR stands next to Victor with a stick in his hand. HE gives guests directions not to get too close. HE allows some guests to pet VICTOR, who reacts shyly and sometimes angrily at the Doctor. COQUETTE discreetly walks by and gives the Doctor an evil glare. The DOCTOR tells her to stay away. VICTOR, calms down and almost touches Coquette, but HE does not look up at her. ARMSTRONG shoots a photo of Victor. The FLASH of light drives VICTOR into a corner. The DOCTOR informs Armstrong that she will not leave the premises with the camera. Excluding Victor, the FOUR OTHER CHARACTERS proceed to mingle and dine with guests after all guests have entered the room, observed Victor and have begun to eat.

First Course: During the first course, CHARACTERS suggest at their tables that someone take Victor some food. COQUETTE brings a plate of food to Victor. VICTOR eats with his fingers, but, for the most part, displays good manners. Only his shy behavior and reactions to the Doctor gives the implication that Victor is primitive. ANNABELLE presses her face against the dining room window during the first course and notices Heinrich and Victor. Her expressions visibly change at seeing them—anger toward Heinrich and sadness toward Victor. CHARACTERS mingle at end of first course. [Director's Note: FRANCES and TWO WAITERS with stretcher on stand-by at end of first course.]

Second Course: Just after the second course begins, the DOCTOR takes his wine glass to the front of the room and gets attention of the guests.

DOCTOR. Ladies and Gentlemen, please join me in a toast. Repeat after me: To Youth! (*Guests repeat.*) To Beauty! (*Repeat.*) To life! (*Repeat.*) To Hell with it all! (*Repeat.—HE drinks wine.*) Absolutely anesthetizing wine! (*Sets glass on podium and puts on spectacles and flips through pages on his clipboard.*) The time has come to reveal my experiment. Right now, between your soup and your salad, history is being made.

(Dracula-type MUSIC begins as the DOCTOR becomes trance-like, and starts speaking like Bela Lugosi.)

DOCTOR. We are about to unfold the story of Von Schtooptenstein, a man of science, who sought to create a human after his own image without ... without ... without? Anyway, it is one of the strangest tales ever told. You are there, a witness to the great mysteries of creation: life and death. I think it will thrill you. It might even horrify you. *(Snaps back to reality.)* Ah ... Ah ... Where was I? All those years I was puzzled by a question. Haunted by a single question, day and night, night and day. If it was possible to transplant two or three detached organs and limbs to a living healthy body, why not graft together a lot of organs, limbs and miscellaneous parts, thereby making an entirely new body from scratch?! So, I said to myself, Von Schtooptenstein, someone tried that and it didn't work out so well. The results of that experiment was Frankenstein's monster and we all know that he destroyed himself, his creator and everything around him. Well, we can't have that, can we? So I'm sitting in my laboratory asking myself why that experiment failed? Why did he destroy himself? I'll tell you why. Because he wasn't pretty to look at. One look in the mirror and it was all over. "Ah hah!", I said. Regenerate old dead tissue on discarded limbs and organs, put it all together, make it look beautiful and you can sell it anywhere. The answer was in the packaging. So, after twenty-five years of research, I have come up with a foolproof secret method to regenerate, re-animate and restructure dead tissue.

ARMSTRONG. Excuse me, Doctor Von Schtooptenstein. Ann Armstrong, *Science News*. You say you've come up with a foolproof method to *(Imitating Doctor.)* regenerate, re-animate and restructure dead tissue after twenty-five years of research. (*Back to her own voice.*) Don't you mean to say that you've come up with a *foolhardy* method after twenty-five years of illegal, faulty and fraudulent *experimentation*?

DOCTOR. Where do you get your information, Miss Armstrong?

ARMSTRONG. Ten years of investigative reporting on you and your organization.

DOCTOR. Spare me the Geraldo Rivera gibberish, Miss Armstrong. I have proof of my work. Reports, pictures. I did nothing illegal.

ARMSTRONG. You have reports and pictures? I'm sure they're headline material for the *National Enquirer*, but I hope you don't expect these people to buy the slop you're feeding them.

DOCTOR. I sure do! I mean, these people can separate fact from fiction.

ARMSTRONG. Science fiction, Doctor. I can see the headlines now, "duped by Doctor Schtoop."

DOCTOR. I am proof that it works. Look at me, my face. I am seventy years old. I don't look a day over seventeen.

ARMSTRONG. So, you've experimented on yourself. Who else have you experimented on Doctor?

DOCTOR. If you would put a cork in that overactive trap of yours, I will bring forward the only other human that I ever experimented on, *with* permission, *perfectly* legally, and *only* on the *epidermal* portions of the body. Down the road, as we prepare for it, my future experiments will take me further when ...

ARMSTRONG. Your past experiments have taken you further. What about that poor man over there. It's inhumane what you're doing to him.

DOCTOR. Inhumane! Him? That, is nature's prank, not mine. And, I intend to reverse the processes of his calamity.

ARMSTRONG. Schtooptenstein the Benevolent. (*SHE sits.*)

DOCTOR. (*Almost under his breath in the direction of Caswell.*) How did she get past security?

(*Stretcher enters with FRANCES lying under a white sheet.*)

WAITER. Hey Buddy, where do you want this?

DOCTOR. The moment has arrived! My *creation* has arrived. Careful with that.

(*Piano plays roll intro to   [cannot use copyrighted music unless you have permission. Please put appropriate substitute here] as underscore.*)

DOCTOR. Bring in the stretcher. This way. Be careful, don't drop her. She is sensitive cargo.

(*ARMSTRONG chases after stretcher and snaps a photo or two.*)

DOCTOR. Armstrong! No photographs, moving pictures or recording devices of any type. Here it is. My singular sensation. My own special creation. I must warn you. No loud or sudden noise or movements. Everyone must try to act as normal as possible. Any distraction may frighten my creation. I will require the help of an able-bodied man to assist in the unveiling. A volunteer whose name will be etched next to mine in the annals of medical journals for all time.

(VOLUNTEER FROM AUDIENCE comes up on stage.)

DOCTOR.   *(To Volunteer.)* What's your name? *(Response.)* How do you feel about this? *(Response.)* Can you handle the shock? *(Response.)* Wait till you see what's under these sheets. She's a humdinger.
ARMSTRONG. Doctor, why a woman?
DOCTOR. I need a helping hand around the laboratory. And I have been lonely since ...

(FRANCES groans.)

DOCTOR. She's awake. Before my assistant and I lift the shroud of Turin ... er ... mystery, I must inform you that the creature's eyes have been bandaged since, you should pardon the expression, birth. They are sensitive to light. They will be closed when she gets up. Maestro, a quiet drum roll please.

(HE lifts the sheet. FRANCES stands with eyes closed and covered with two cotton balls. Her arms are out in front of her.)

DOCTOR. Ladies and gentlemen, I give you Frances.

(FRANCES bows.)

DOCTOR. She is reacting already. Now there is a very strong possibility that when I remove the cotton balls from her eyes that whatever and whoever the creature sees first, it, she, she will fixate or attach itself to! So please stay in your seats everyone. I will make sure it only looks at me for the first time. This is it! If you feel squeamish or do not care to subject your nerves to such a strain, leave the room, 'cause I warned you.

(*HE removes cotton balls. FRANCES opens her eyes, looks at the Doctor, looks at the volunteer, looks forward, turns body to and hugs volunteer.*)

FRANCES. Daddy. (*Points to self.*) Frances. (*Points to volunteer.*) Daddy.
DOCTOR. Frances, my creation!
FRANCES. (*Turning to Doctor.*) Who are you?
DOCTOR. Frances, don't you know me? I am Heinrich Von Schtooptenstein, M.D., Ph.D., V.D. I conceived, constructed, reshaped and erected you from dead tissue.
FRANCES. Listen buster, I wasn't born yesterday. You didn't conceive, construct or erect anything. And can't you see I'm busy here with ... (*To Volunteer while curling the hairs on his head.*) What's your name big boy?
DOCTOR. Frances lie down, you're in shock.
FRANCES. (*To Volunteer.*) Ain't it always like a man to ask a woman to lie down before they're familiar with one another. So, what'd'ya say, you wanna go for a ride on my stretcher? See what we can conceive, construct ...
DOCTOR. Frances, I'll have none of that!
FRANCES. You're right this time Doc cause I ain't offerin' you none of *that*!
DOCTOR. I see that your mind and your mouth work just fine. Now, let go of that man, Frances, we must conduct a few tests on you for the benefit of our audience. Now look straight ahead.
FRANCES. Audience! Tests! Listen, Doc, unless I'm gettin' union rates, you ain't gettin' no song and dance out of this broad.
DOCTOR. Would you mind answering a few questions from our guests?

FRANCES. One or two, and make it quick, those cotton balls did a number on my lashes, and this frock is not my color.
DOCTOR. Do any of our distinguished guests have a question for Frances?

(*They receive questions.*)

FRANCES. Doc, I am indebted to you for the home improvements but, I'm hungry and I'd like to know what I'm supposed to do with the rest of my life.

(*HE dangles a watch in front of her eyes. SHE goes into a trance with eyes closed and arms out in front of her.*)

DOCTOR. Hypnosis. A little insurance. Frances, can you hear me?
FRANCES. Yes, sir.
DOCTOR. Frances, from now on, you are going to be my assistant.
FRANCES. Your assistant, sir.
DOCTOR. My nurse.
FRANCES. Your nurse, sir.
DOCTOR. You will address me as Doctor.
FRANCES. Yes, Doctor.
DOCTOR. And you will obey my every direction.
FRANCES. Say what? (*He will instruct her to touch her nose and she'll touch her breast. He'll instruct her to clap her hands and she'll clap her knees together.*)
DOCTOR. The mind can only absorb so much. That's enough for today Frances. When I count to three you will snap out of it. You will remember nothing in the past, only my directions. Is that clear?
FRANCES. Yes, Doctor.
DOCTOR. One, two, three.

FRANCES. (*Wakes up and is more authoritative than ever. To Volunteer.*) Come with me sailor, nurseykins is gonna take your temperature.

(*As SHE escorts him off stage, VICTOR groans.*)

FRANCES. Oh Doctor, this poor thing is in pain. Speak to Mamma. Oh look, (*Referring to his water bowl.*) His bedpan is full. I'll empty it.

(*VICTOR groans.*)

FRANCES. Don't get so huffy. Do you want to go to the latrine? Nurse will take you.
VICTOR. Out! Out!
FRANCES. Oh, you want to do it outside in the bushes. I can understand. Ok, ok! I'll take you out to the bushes to do your business. (*FRANCES unhooks chain.*)
DOCTOR. Frances! You can't handle him.
FRANCES. There ain't a man Frances can't handle.
DOCTOR. Besides, it is not safe.
FRANCES. I promise, I won't let him lay a hand on me.
DOCTOR. It isn't him I'm worried about.
FRANCES. I beg your pardon!
DOCTOR. It isn't ... it just isn't safe.
FRANCES. Don't go gettin' your ruffles all wrinkled, Heiney, we're goin'. Let's go, Slugger. When we come back I'll feed you a nice bowl of Kibbles and Bits.

(*FRANCES exits with VICTOR on chain leash. CHARACTERS mix.*)

Scene 3

(*Soon after the main course is served, ANNABELLE and COQUETTE exit separately upon cue. The gun is kept on stand-by. The DOCTOR has a small blood packet in a tissue in his hand and the eye patch in his lab coat. FRANCES returns all dishevelled with dirt on her face, chain in tow.*)

FRANCES. Someone help me! Help! Doctor, doctor!

DOCTOR. Your lungs are very functional, Frances.

FRANCES. Forget Frances' functional lungs. Help me. I have been violated.

DOCTOR. Raped?

FRANCES. No chance.

DOCTOR. That ... that thing did this to you. I knew I shouldn't have let you ...

FRANCES. That's no way to talk about a former patient.

DOCTOR. Former patient? Where is he?

FRANCES. What am I chopped liver? My person was just brutally violated and you want to know where Lurch is?

DOCTOR. Stop babbling and tell me what happened.

FRANCES. I was attached by a shrub.

DOCTOR. A shrub?

FRANCES. Your hearing's intact. A shrub. Maybe two shrubs. Or someone hiding in a shrub. I don't know. I was hit over the head with a hard object. I fell on the ground, hence the dirt on my face. I woke up. Lurch was gone, maybe kidnapped ... beastnapped. He left behind these (*Holds up chains.*) and a puddle of piddle out by the shrubs.

DOCTOR. Did he hit you?

FRANCES. I don't know who hit me. Maybe he was kidnapped. We ought to call the police.

DOCTOR. No. That won't be necessary.
FRANCES. Yes, Doctor. I'm going to get cleaned up, rearrange my face and ... (*SHE exits.*)

(*As SHE exits SHE passes COQUETTE returning.*)

DOCTOR. You'll rearrange nothing! I'll do any rearranging if there's rearranging to do. Ladies and Gentlemen, I am so sorry to have disturbed your meal. Our little symposium has lost one of it's principal objects, or should I say subjects, for presentation. My presentation on advanced tissue regeneration, which I was saving for dessert, was my most challenging endeavor. To take that creature from the depths of despair and restore beauty has been something that I have dreamt about for years. At this time, I would humbly like to ask some of you to volunteer to join a search party to find the missing subject.

(*A GUNSHOT sounds and the DOCTOR is hit in the eye. COQUETTE and FRANCES, nearby, both SCREAM. The DOCTOR quickly grabs his eye with the hand that holds the tissue and blood packet. Blood oozes through his fingers and down his face. Director's Note: Use just enough blood not to run onto lab coat and/or make sure Doctor uses a napkin around his neck at dinner, and leaves it on for gunshot.*
DOCTOR ad-libs much pain. He's a sissy when it comes to blood, especially his own. CASWELL, keeping the flow of action going, pulls his gun, aims it in the direction of the gunshot, runs to the Doctor's side and takes over. By now, ARMSTRONG and FRANCES are back in the room. FRANCES is wearing a nurse's cap. ARMSTRONG calls for someone to get an ambulance and the police. WAITERS take the DOCTOR out of the room on a stretcher.)

CASWELL. Everyone calm down. There's no need to call anyone. Where are they taking him?

FRANCES. We have a little infirmary set-up in the pantry. On these symposiums you never know when it's necessary to do a little on the spot (*Imitating the Doctor's accent.*) reshaping, reorganizing and re-animating. Hey! Who are you?

CASWELL. Caswell Huddlestone.

FRANCES. Since you're carrying the gun, I'll buy that.

(*Fast paced and heated exchange. HE keeps gun pointed at arms length.*)

ARMSTRONG. I won't buy it so easily. Ann Armstrong, Mr. Huddlestone.

CASWELL. I know all about you, Miss Armstrong.

ARMSTRONG. You do? Well *we* don't know about you, so, why don't you tell us?

CASWELL. You journalists are quick to claim to be part of the majority. I'd say you are among the slightly insignificant minority here tonight.

ARMSTRONG. You're avoiding the question Huddlestone. Who are you?

CASWELL. It's not a crime to avoid a question. It could be a crime to appear on the scene just after a shooting.

ARMSTRONG. Who are you? Why are you pointing that gun at me? And why hasn't someone called the police? (*HE drops gun to his side.*)

CASWELL. Forget the police. I'm a Federal marshal. (*Flips badge.*) You answer the questions now. Where were you when the Doctor was shot?

ARMSTRONG. On the telephone.

CASWELL. Can you prove it?

(*LOUIE and ANNABELLE enter singing, from the hallway
    with bags and a bottle of booze appearing happy and
    very sauced.*
*THEY both break into a happy long laugh as THEY
    stumble through the room. Their laughing carries on
    into their dialogue.*)

ANNABELLE. Oh, Louie, you keep me in stitches.
Hey, are we late for supper?
    LOUIE. We brung the bottle.
    ANNABELLE. So whose got the beef?

(*THEY both laugh.*)

LOUIE. Annie, they look serious. Cheer up! There ain't
no meet'n without me an my Annie Belle. And we're here.

(*THEY both grab some food from a table, ever so politely
    by saying "May I?", and proceed to eat it and talk.*)

ANNABELLE. Moonbeam, are we in the right place?
    LOUIE. Yes, my honey, the sign in the hallway says
we're where we're supposed to be.
    ARMSTRONG. Louie, you can't read.
    LOUIE. Here they are. Here we are. We're here.
    ANNABELLE. A philosopher you ain't.
    FRANCES. (*Enters.*) Oh, Mr. Fed, sir. Nurse Frances
with an update on the ailing Doctor, he's gonna be ...
(*Notices Annabelle and Louie.*) Whoa! Where'd they get
you two? There's not a subway around for miles. (*To
Annabelle.*) Lurch, meet your mother! Honey, the
emergency room's that way. And we're out of spare parts
for the weekend.

LOUIE. (*Looking at Frances.*) Annie, get a load a that. You're lookin' better every day.

ANNABELLE. (*Looking at Frances.*) Louie, we gotta stop drinkin' this stuff. My eyes is playin' tricks on me. Vamoose. (*THEY start to exit, vaudeville steps.*)

LOUIE. I'm right behind you.

CASWELL. (*Deadpan.*) Don't move you two.

(*THEY both turn around and smile.*)

ANNABELLE. (*Southern petite accent.*) Whatever do you mean, kind sir? Why, my friend and I were just about to join you all for tea.

(*LOUIE holds out his arm as SHE does a minuet turn and curtsey.*)

CASWELL. Your names?

ANNABELLE. (*French accent.*) I am Madame Le Prince de Beaumont, s'il vous plait.

LOUIE. (*French accent.*) Louie the Fourteenth at your beck and call.

CASWELL. Where do you live?

ANNABELLE. Sixteen hundred Pennsylvania Avenue. Drop in. Visit us. We got plenty of extra beds. Louie here is special adviser to the President on unemployment.

LOUIE. Oh, yes. Things are lookin' good for the economy. Did you know that there are seventy-five million homeless people on the streets right now. But that's ok cause employment's up. Eatin's down. But *we* are gonna change that.

DOCTOR. (*Enters with a patch on his eye.*) Mr. Huddlestone, Ladies and Gentlemen, I was just grazed.

(*ANNABELLE and HEINRICH are face to face. Dramatic take with underscore.*)

ANNABELLE. Come on Louie, we have an appointment. Besides it's startin' to smell like a hospital in here and you know how I hate hospitals.

DOCTOR. What's going on here? What are they doing here?

CASWELL. Hold on Doctor Von Schtooptenstein. (*To Annie and Louie.*) And you two, join the party. I want to search your bags.

ANNABELLE. You want to search my bags? Be my guest, Mr. Fed. You better bring a search warrant. Them's my bags. And you better bring in the reinforcements else you'll grow old searching for something in them bags.

CASWELL. I've got some questions for some of you in this room. The attempted murder of the doctor and the probable kidnapping are my job now. I'll explain more to you later, if I think you're ready to hear it. No one leaves this place. No one makes any phone calls without my permission. I'll be back. Carry on.

Scene 4

CASWELL. Ladies and gentlemen. I regret that your symposium has been disturbed by a kidnapper and sniper. I searched the area where the creature was last seen.

FRANCES. Excuse me, sir. You say you searched the area where the creature was last seen?

CASWELL. That's correct.

FRANCES. Which creature might you be referring to? My retinas may be retreads, but I clearly see a number of *creatures*, including myself, roaming these premises.

CASWELL. I'm referring to the creature no longer roaming these premises. I found at least three, possibly four sets of foot prints near the site of the abduction. There are no dragging footprints on the ground, so we know that the nurse was the only creature that was knocked out at the time of the kidnapping. For what it's worth, the bullet that grazed Doctor Von Schtooptenstein was shot from a Saturday night special. Without a warrant, I was unable to search the satchels of Annabelle, the bag lady. I am attempting to establish who else possesses a gun, a motive for the kidnapping and the attempted murder of Doctor Von Schtoopstein. Aside from the missing creature and an unfriendly reporter, I have yet to sort out who might prefer the Doctor to join the ranks of inert tissue. You are a scientific group, of sorts. Therefore, I would like to give you the opportunity right now to ask a few questions of your own to me or to anyone in this room. Are there any questions?

(*HE fields questions, if any, for no more than five minutes. Near the end of the Q&A, the DOCTOR interrupts and offers a reward for the return of the beast. The REPORTER reacts angrily. LOUIE quietly smiles.*)

DOCTOR. If there are no more questions, I would like to remind you that you are all suspect until we resolve the crimes committed here tonight. There is at least one trigger happy snipper among us or roaming the neighborhood. So no one leave the premises without my permission. Please travel in pairs and double lock your door. Pleasant dreams.

(*On weekend events, LOUIE and ANNIE lead the crowd, ad-lib, in some sing-a-longs. ANNIE pulls handouts from one of her bags and LOUIE distributes them. NOTE: ANNIE and HEINRICH are wearing similar wedding bands. Annie's is often hidden under her tattered glove, but is noticeable nonetheless.)*

Physical Clues found on Friday evening and announced by Detective:

1. On the bathroom mirrors: Blood is thicker than bourbon.
2. Rhyme written on the page of a coloring book: a beast of a man meets a beauty of a woman, the clue is the link between the two.

Scene 5

As guests arrive in the dining room, ANNABELLE is sound asleep snoring, tossing and turning in their ready-made cardboard box apartments. LOUIE arrives and mixes with the guests, then falls asleep beside her. As the scene progresses, until their cue to wake up, THEY groan and react to dialogue, and, occasionally throw in a word or two. Entrances: COQUETTE, ARMSTRONG, CASWELL, and FRANCES. THEY work the crowd as they dine. FRANCES ad-libs over the bodies of Louie and Annabelle. She is wearing a nurse's uniform and cap and carries an oversized tongue depressor and enema bag.
Upon cue, DOCTOR enters with VICTOR in chains. CASWELL goes to center stage.

DOCTOR. Frances! Help me. Get in there before I beat you to within an inch of your life.
VICTOR. Arrrgh!
CASWELL. Where did you find him?

VICTOR. Arrrrgh!

DOCTOR. He won't tell me. But, I'll get it out of him. I know what hurts him.

CASWELL. Doctor, please.

FRANCES. Oh my God, it's Lurch. Where have you been? Didn't you get a wake up call?

VICTOR. Arrrgh!

FRANCES. You don't have to tell me! The service in this place is a bit lax.

VICTOR. Arrrgh!

FRANCES. Tell me about it. Sit down and we'll get you some breakfasts. It's too late for room service. But you gotta eat. It'll loosen the vocal chords. Ain't that right Herr Doctor? You're not human till you have your coffee and some breakfast. How about a nice bowl of steroids ... the breakfast of olympic champions. (*SHE tucks napkin in his shirt.*)

VICTOR. Arrgh!

FRANCES. What, you don't feel hungry? What's the matter? I just love protruding foreheads.

VICTOR. Arrrgh! (*HE stands with big gesture.*)

FRANCES. Talk to Frances. What happened to you last night?

VICTOR. Arrrrgh!

FRANCES. You want to play charades. I love charades. Sounds like? First syllable?

(*VICTOR signals baby. Rocking motion with arms.*)

FRANCES. Baby. Now we're gettin' somewhere. You feel like a baby. You want Frances to hold you like a baby.

(*VICTOR is on knees, sucks thumb, groans.*)

FRANCES. You've been a bad boy. You want Frances to spank you.

(*VICTOR points finger, shakes finger at Frances.*)

FRANCES. You want to spank Frances. Maybe later.

(*VICTOR gestures small with his fingers.*)

FRANCES. Well not if it's small, forget it.
VICTOR. Arrrgh! (*Gestures small child.*)
FRANCES. Oh, small baby. (*To audience.*) Can anyone help me? (*SHE directs audience attempts to solve it, then SHE butts in.*) You're not a little boy anymore, it's time to learn to talk already. You're gettin' my goat.
VICTOR. Arrrrggh!
FRANCES. Goat. Kid. Little boy. Kid. I get it. Second syllable, sounds like.

(*VICTOR slaps her.*)

FRANCES. Don't you slap me in that tone of voice.
VICTOR. Arrgggh!
FRANCES. Slap. Kid slap.

(*VICTOR gestures up alphabet sign.*)

FRANCES. Kid nap. You were kidnapped! We know you were kidnapped Einstein. These people have to leave in a few hours. Who kidnapped you?

(*VICTOR points to a woman with blonde hair.*)

FRANCES. That lady kidnapped you?

(VICTOR shakes his head "no." Points to her hair.)

FRANCES. This lady's hair kidnapped you. You were kidnapped by a wig.
VICTOR. Arrrgh! *(HE touches her hair.)*
FRANCES. A cheap blonde kidnapped you.

(VICTOR covers his eyes.)

FRANCES. You don't want to look at her. Well, I can see why. Honey, take my advice, go for the natural look, like me. Earth tones.

(VICTOR covers his eyes and touches her hair, then pulls at his ear.)

FRANCES. Can't see. Blonde. Sounds like. Blind.

(ANNABELLE wakes up and observes silently.)

COQUETTE. *(Very excitable and upset.)* Excuse me, miss, pardon me, I have been standing around watching this foolishness for too long.
FRANCES. Please to meet you too. The name's Frances.
COQUETTE. That's no way to communicate with him.
FRANCES. Honey, I barely got a word in edge-wise. He nearly talked my ears off, and they're on loan.
COQUETTE. Kindness responds to kindness. Don't push him.
FRANCES. Another authority on bestial relations.
COQUETTE. He responds to me.
FRANCES. I should try more cleavage.
COQUETTE. He has feelings, you know.

FRANCES. Feelings! He's yours, honey. He's cute, but dumb. All meat and no potatoes. You two belong together.

DOCTOR. They do not belong together! They will not be together! (*Cracks whip.*) Never! Never! I won't have it!

COQUETTE. Stay out of this, Father.

DOCTOR. You called me Father.

COQUETTE. Victor, it's me, Coquette. Don't you recognize me? (*SHE takes his hand.*) I know it's been a while. (*A love theme underscore plays during Victor/Coquette dialogue.*)

VICTOR. (*Struggling gently to speak.*) Coquette, Coquette.

COQUETTE. I'm here Victor.

VICTOR. Stay with me.

COQUETTE. Who kidnapped you?

VICTOR. I was blindfolded ... wasn't hurt ... deal with...

DOCTOR. (*To Caswell.*) Stop them.

CASWELL. This is all very interesting, your little love scene, Miss Von Schtooptenstein. But not so convincing, I'm afraid.

COQUETTE. He's telling the truth.

VICTOR. No Coquette. Say no more. "If we speak we are condemned. If we are silent we are damned."

FRANCES. Poetic. Very poetic.

CASWELL. Poetry does not cut it here.

COQUETTE. Deception does, doesn't it, Detective ... whatever you are.

ARMSTRONG. Yes, what is your relationship to the doctor and this organization, Mr. Huddlestone?

CASWELL. Don't you know, Miss Armstrong?

ARMSTRONG. I have my theories. And when I find out ...

DOCTOR. Watch it or we'll slap you with another libel suit Miss Armstrong.

ARMSTRONG. Very schmart Von Schtooptenstein. You got it and you'll get it.

CASWELL. Everyone, sit down. In answer to the reporter's query, I will tell you that the United States government has a keen interest in the research of Doctor Von Schtooptenstein and that of the Society. We are aware that his work is highly sensitive.

(*VICTOR groans.*)

CASWELL. Hence, my presence. Now a sniper and kidnapper are still at large. This *kidnapping*, may have been a set-up, maybe not. The return of Victor we've yet to have explained. And, Victor's role in this matter is still a mystery.

ARMSTRONG. That's a very clear summary, Marshal. However, someone must *investigate* this mess. And so far, all you've done is tell us about it. I'd like to follow up some questioning right now from last night. It's about the gun. You didn't question anyone in much detail whether or not guests were carrying a gun. I want to ask a few people. First, Annabelle. Do you carry a gun?

ANNABELLE. Yeah, sure, I possess a gun. A lady needs protection and the only thing Louis can box is oranges.

ARMSTRONG. Annabelle, is your gun a Saturday night special?

ANNABELLE. I don't know, but right here (*SHE pulls out a styrofoam dinner container.*) I got a Wednesday night special from the stage delicatessen. Corn beef on rye. Only four days old. You want some?

ARMSTRONG. No thank you. I've eaten.

ANNABELLE. I'll save it for later. A midday snack. Hey, do you own a gun Miss Smartypants?

ARMSTRONG. As a matter of fact I do. It's in the glove compartment of my automobile.

LOUIE. The '87 Mercedes parked outside?

ARMSTRONG. Yes, why?

LOUIE. Sleeps two very comfortably.

CASWELL. Miss Armstrong, is your gun a Saturday night special?

ARMSTRONG. Might be.

CASWELL. Ladies and gentlemen, at this time, some of you may ask questions of the reporter or others in this happy gathering.

(THEY receive questions. If the audience doesn't force the Detective and Doctor to release Victor, then ARMSTRONG does. The Detective wraps-up with the schedule for the remainder of the day.)

Optional Scene 6

1. A discreet argument between Annabelle and Coquette regarding Coquette's relationship with Victor. Coquette still does not recognize her mother; and

2. Coquette and Victor solidifying their love relationship.

If there is no afternoon high tea, Director includes these ad libs into Saturday cocktails. Also, throughout the event segments of the following limericks are hidden to be found by guests.

Limericks

THERE ONCE WAS A FAIR PAIR
WHO WERE ALTERED WITHOUT CARE
JUST ONE CHILD
STAYED OH SO WILD
AND THE OTHER LONGS FOR THE LAIR

MEMORIES OF SOME KIN ARE GONE
AND TOGETHER THE TWO ARE DRAWN
KNOWING THE WRONG
THE REASON IS STRONG
TO REMOVE THE INNOCENT PAWN

CHARGING A RANSOM
CAN SURELY LAND SOME
WHEN THEY OUGHTTA
REALIZE THE WORD IS MUM

Scene 7

Parade of Suspects

Cocktails and dinner on Saturday evening can be in costume.

CHARACTERS mix during the initial part of the cocktail period. COQUETTE arrives with VICTOR.

During the last twenty to twenty-five minutes of cocktails, CASWELL conducts the Parade of Suspects. HE explains the bribes and that the bribe money will be at each of their place settings at dinner.

During parade, Louie is discovered stabbed to death under a table. His bloody arm falls out from under the table onto a guest's foot. One of his shoes is off. Money is stuffed deep in the shoe for guests to find.

ANNABELLE. (*Weeps and wails.*) Louie we never win, you and me. You son of a bitch. I was countin' on ya. You were my last hope and you let me down. You always thought you could pull the wool over my eyes. I always knew, Moonbeam. Always. Another day, another dollar, another destiny. Don't worry Louie, you're goin' to heaven. St. Peter was a pauper, too. And he guards the pearly gates. Save me a spot, old buddy.

(*CASWELL takes control of event.*)

Questions for the "Parade of Suspects"

(*Questions or general questioning categories are outlined below. Note to actors: paraphrase and embellish the outline below except for Annabelle's Q. and A.*)

CASWELL. Annabelle, please come forward. I have a few questions for you. I realize that this is a difficult time for you.
ANNABELLE. Not as difficult a time as it's gonna be for you.
CASWELL. May I suggest that it would be to your advantage to cooperate with me.
ANNABELLE. No, you may not suggest that it would be to my advantage to cooperate with you. When I want your opinion I'll ask for it.
CASWELL. Don't push me. It's only *you* that will pay in the end.
ANNABELLE. I been payin' *in the end* all my life. So tell me somethin' new.
CASWELL. I don't want to tell you anything, I only want some straight answers.
ANNABELLE. Shoot, Copper.

CASWELL. What's your last name?

ANNABELLE. It don't matter. Most people don't even wanna know my first.

CASWELL. What's your last name?

ANNABELLE. I'm bereaved. Don't push it.

CASWELL. What was Louie's last name?

ANNABELLE. I never asked.

CASWELL. What do you mean you never asked?

ANNABELLE. Right over your head. Look at me. Look out there. Look at you. What is wrong with this picture? Where I come from, other things are important.

CASWELL. This is important. Your friend is dead. And I'm trying to find his killer. Or is he your friend?

ANNABELLE. What are you gettin' at?

CASWELL. How would you characterize your relationship with Louie?

ANNABELLE. (*Stonewalling.*) Bag man and bag lady.

CASWELL. Were you very close?

ANNABELLE. When two people live in a refrigerator box, believe me, your close.

CASWELL. How close?

ANNABELLE. You mean was I gettin' any? (*Pause.*) My activities in the bedroom ain't government business and they sure ain't gonna solve Louie's murder.

CASWELL. How long have you known Louie?

ANNABELLE. Let me see. I ain't good with dates. Can't never remember dates. Would like to forget most of 'em. Me and Louie met ... let's see ... what's his name was president ... Ah ... was it the crook with the big nose? Noooo. It was when that son of a bitch millionaire with the oil wells resided in the white house.

CASWELL. Well that could be any one of a dozen presidents.

ANNABELLE. (*Shoots him a look.*) No! No! You know, the one married to the Byrd brain.

CASWELL. Well that could be any one of a dozen presidents.

ANNABELLE. Read ... my ... lips, Caswell. Lady ... *Byrd*! Everyone in the house was named after a byrd. And these people was runnin' the country.

CASWELL. (*Impatient.*) Are you saying LBJ was president when you met Louie?

ANNABELLE. Imagine, what mother in her right mind would name her kids Lynda Byrd and Lucy Byrd?

CASWELL. (*On the offensive.*) Annabelle, you seem to have a lot of outspoken political opinions. I'll bet you don't even vote. Do you?

ANNABELLE. Not in over twenty years. I turned off, turned out and retired from civilization back about then.

CASWELL. (*Suggestive.*) Drugs?

ANNABELLE. (*Angry.*) I don't believe in abusin' the body, Caswell. Not like hippies. Not like this here Society for the Advancement of Artificial Beauty. Not like the government that experiments on the innocent. What I do is totally "au natural," ain't that right Lou ... Louie? (*Cries and shakes her head.*) Ah, Louie.

CASWELL. Speakin' of Louie.

ANNABELLE. I don't wanna talk about Louie no more.

CASWELL. Did Louie have a record?

ANNABELLE. Naaaaa, he couldn't sing, or should I say, he ain't singin' no more.

CASWELL. A criminal record.

ANNABELLE. Louie was an honest man. Maybe a little weak, maybe a little petty larceny, but an honest man. *I*, was the only one that ever worried about Louie. *I*, kept people from takin' advantage of him. I take ... took care of Louie. Don't *you* say nothin' about my Louie. I'll kick your ass from here to kingdom come. (*SHE slaps him in the face.*)

CASWELL. Settle down. Settle down. I'm finished with you ... for now. Let this crowd take a shot at you, if they're ready. Are there any questions for the next heavyweight champion?

(*Audience Q&A.*)

(*ARMSTRONG is questioned by CASWELL regarding the libel suit.*
CASWELL begins to question VICTOR. VICTOR resists Caswell. CASWELL lets audience question Victor. VICTOR answers several questions then runs out of the room in disgust, saying "no more."
COQUETTE and HEINRICH are questioned about their relationship. COQUETTE calls her father a liar. COQUETTE announces that she and Victor will be married. HEINRICH protests as COQUETTE insists and exits saying that he cannot stop them. ARMSTRONG interrupts.)

ARMSTRONG. Doctor, let's talk science for a minute. You spoke of the theory of relativity in your research. You spoke of unpredictable change and mutability in your Nobel prize pitch yesterday. That means some loss of control in time and space to obtain your results.
DOCTOR. Yes.
ARMSTRONG. Does that also mean that in your research you sometimes lose experimental control, results don't always go the way you want?
DOCTOR. (*Hedging.*) Ah ... er ... my results always go the way I want.
ARMSTRONG. Don't you sometimes manipulate those results?
DOCTOR. I do no such thing.

ARMSTRONG. And you manipulate your research notes?

DOCTOR. You need a doctor. You're unstable Miss Armstrong. I do not manipulate my research.

ARMSTRONG. How about your experiments? Your "subjects"?

DOCTOR. My subjects are dead tissue!

ARMSTRONG. Are they dead, Doctor?

DOCTOR. Yes, dead.

ARMSTRONG. Your definition of death and inertia is insensitive to the human condition.

DOCTOR. I don't have to listen to this. I've got to prepare my speech for tonight. Excuse me.

(HEINRICH exits. DETECTIVE entertains a few questions for Armstrong and closes Q and A. session.)

Scene 8

Bribe clues

DOCTOR—Louie's achille's tells a part of the story.
COQUETTE—I never remember a face.
ANNABELLE—You always hurt the ones you love.
FRANCES. In a crazy, mixed-up world, love destroys.
VICTOR—I forgive both.

(Director's Note: If audience needs more time to ask questions, Parade of Suspects can continue into dinner. CHARACTERS work crowd during dinner. ANNABELLE is noticed drinking heavily from her bottle. At one point, COQUETTE and VICTOR go out hand in hand for a walk. The REPORTER exits, ANNABELLE exits and the DOCTOR exits. GUNSHOTS ring out.

Dramatic MUSIC underscore. COQUETTE screams and returns bloodied with VICTOR stumbling into room after her. HE dies near her. feet. ARMSTRONG and FRANCES comfort Coquette. ANNABELLE quietly cries in the corner. COQUETTE physically attacks and blames her father. CASWELL finds a picture of baby (on back of photo are initials "VS") on the body of Victor. CASWELL takes over. Ad-libbed scene with Q&A. Resolution forms are handed out with instructions for completion and submission.

Scene 9

Resolution

CASWELL. Ladies and Gentlemen. It is time to resolve these heinous crimes. We have quite a mess to sort out. First, the kidnapping and subsequent bloody murder of Victor. Second, the attempted murder of Doctor Von Schtooptenstein. And finally, the brutal stabbing death of Louie, the bag man. After consideration of the facts, review of circumstantial evidence, and listening very carefully to the testimony of many very strange characters, I now know who the killer is.

Yes, there was one killer. But, not always acting alone. And God knows, more people than just the killer are guilty—because they helped cause the killing. I may not be able to prove that in a court of law, because only the killer pulled the trigger and twisted the knife. You see, if I were not an arm of the law, I would say that this is a case where the killer killed for all the right reasons.

Let's start with the kidnapping of Victor. Who did it and why? Was it the mad doctor?

DOCTOR. I object to that remark!

CASWELL. Overruled. Sit down or I'll have you tied down!

CASWELL. Victor, Ladies and Gentlemen, was kidnapped for the same reason he was killed. As the limerick said: To remove the innocent pawn. To protect him from fate, from everything, from everyone, from experimentation ...

DOCTOR. You're crazy!

CASWELL. No, I'm not crazy, Doctor. You have cornered that market.

DOCTOR. Such abuse!

CASWELL. You haven't seen abuse. Stick around.

DOCTOR. Bureaucrats! You give them a badge, a gun and a little power, and see what happens to them.

CASWELL. You truly are insane. Frances. Gag him.

FRANCES. My pleasure. (*SHE ties a dinner napkin around his mouth.*)

CASWELL. Where was I? So who had a motive to kidnap Victor? Von Schtooptenstein wanted Victor for his experiments. He wouldn't have done it. Frances.

FRANCES. (*SHE steps forward.*) Are you speaking to "moi"?

CASWELL. You were servile to the demanding doctor.

FRANCES. Servant! Well I wouldn't put it quite that way, but go on.

CASWELL. Maybe you kidnapped Victor. Maybe you wanted to get a little revenge for the Doctor turning you into "that."

FRANCES. Listen here, Caswell. Firstly, I couldn't have kidnapped him. I had just been hypnotized by the Doctor to serve him. Hypnosis is a very powerful psychological tool. And I was under the influence of that tool. Secondly, I happen to like "this." You may not, but it's all that I've got. (*To guest.*) You believe me don't you?

CASWELL. I believe you, Frances.

FRANCES. Thank you.

CASWELL. Let's get back to the kidnapping. Miss Armstrong. (*SHE stands*.) You wanted the Doctor's experimenting to stop. There's also the libel suit that might have motivated a little revenge. And you were out of the room when it happened. Were you responsible for his kidnapping?

ARMSTRONG. You know better, Huddlestone. I'm an investigative reporter. If I break the law, I lose my story on the mad scientist (*DOCTOR groans*.) and I'm not about to do that. Why don't you look to the obvious protector of Victor. Coquette Von Schtooptenstein.

COQUETTE. (*Stands*.) Leave me out of this!

ARMSTRONG. Come on cutesy. You loved him. You were out of the room. You kidnapped him.

COQUETTE. I didn't. I couldn't. I wanted to. But, I couldn't have done it all alone. I'd have needed help.

ARMSTRONG. So, someone helped you do it.

COQUETTE. Who? I didn't know anyone here, except my father.

ARMSTRONG. I don't believe you.

CASWELL. I do. Yes, two people kidnapped Victor. But let me digress again for a minute. Coquette, you know more than you have been telling us.

COQUETTE. What do you mean?

CASWELL. Your father's experimentation was the cause of all of this mess. And you did not speak up. Why?

COQUETTE. Would you believe me if I said "The cat's got my tongue"?

CASWELL. I've watched you closely. You have displayed unusual mannerisms this weekend. Animal mannerisms.

COQUETTE. It's from hanging around Victor.

CASWELL. No, it's because your father experimented on you. Just like Victor.

COQUETTE. No! He didn't.

CASWELL. Yes he did. You were one of the "Fair Pair" that the Doctor "altered" "without care." Armstrong's questioning in the Parade of Suspects helped me. You were one of your father's experiments. He turned you into a beast when you were a child. Then he turned you back into a beauty. Isn't that correct?

COQUETTE. Yes. Yes. (*SHE breaks down.*)

CASWELL. And you weren't the only one he experimented on twenty some years ago. How about the other member of the "Fair Pair"? Victor. The picture of the baby we found on Victor's dead body was Victor as a child, as a normal child. Your father turned Victor into a beast.

COQUETTE. He's not a beast. He's beautiful. My father should have let us both be. We were happy. I loved him. But he prevented us from being together.

CASWELL. The clue is the link between the two. He did that because Victor was your brother.

(*COQUETTE gasps.*)

CASWELL. The initials "VS" were on the back of that picture. Victor Von Schtooptenstein. You were in love with your twin brother.

COQUETTE. Oh no!

CASWELL. Oh yes!

FRANCES. Oh, so sick!

CASWELL. The experiments altered your memory. And you didn't know about Victor. You were duped by your father.

COQUETTE. But I don't understand. I didn't kidnap Victor. I didn't kill Victor.

ANNABELLE. (*Enters carrying a gun pointed at the audience. She is dressed up.*) I did.

COQUETTE. What? You? Why?

ANNABELLE. Tell her, Caswell.

CASWELL. Blood is thicker than bourbon. Anna Von Schtooptenstein.

DOCTOR. (*Rips off gag.*) My wife!

COQUETTE. My mother!

FRANCES. My God!

CASWELL. You left your children twenty-two years ago. Dropped out of sight.

ANNABELLE. I couldn't take it. I had to leave. He destroyed our family. But when I saw what he had done to my Victor. That was enough!

CASWELL. So you and Louie kidnapped Victor.

ANNABELLE. Louie. The poor dope. He didn't know what he was going on.

CASWELL. And you took a shot at Heinrich.

ANNABELLE. An eye for an eye.

CASWELL. And you stabbed Louie!

ANNABELLE. He was weak. He got in my way. He brought Victor back to Heinrich for the reward. I had to kill him.

CASWELL. And your son, Victor?

ANNABELLE. My son. I couldn't let him go through any more torture.

COQUETTE. Mother, how could you?

ANNABELLE. I couldn't let you marry him.

COQUETTE. How could you leave us? We were your children. Why didn't you tell me?

ANNABELLE. I was weak. And what good would it have done to tell you? You were small children then. But not anymore. And I'm not weak anymore. And there's one thing I should have done twenty-two years ago. It's the end of the line, Heinrich von Schtooptenstein.!

(SHE shoots the Doctor twice. HE dies.)

ANNABELLE. I'm sorry Coquette. I love you. *(ANNABELLE turns the gun on herself.)*
CASWELL. No!
COQUETTE. Noooo! *(SHE runs toward her mother and is stopped midway by the sound of the GUNSHOT.)*

(ANNABELLE dies.)

CASWELL. There you have it, ladies and gentlemen, "Beauty Meets the Beast."

Curtain Call
Awards
End

ORGAN DONOR CARD

SOCIETY FOR THE ADVANCEMENT OF BEAUTY THROUGH TISSUE RESEARCH

DONOR CANDIDATE CARD

Donor Name______________________________

Yes, I would like to contribute to the
Society. Please take
my:______________________________
____
____
____

No, I have nothing to donate to the
Society. But I could use some extra
parts:
____
____
____

COSTUME AND PROP LIST

Lab coat (Doctor)
ID tag (Doctor)
Stethoscope
Rubber gloves
(2) Boxes of tissues
Enema bag
Tongue depressors (box)
Pajamas (Doctor)
Doctor's head reflector (optional)
Bag lady bag stuffed with accessories
.22 gun (Annabelle) (starter)
(2) Empty booze bottles (Annabelle and Louie)
Hats for bag lady and man
Matching wedding rings (Heinrich and Annabelle)
Black teeth wax (Louie and Annabelle)
Packet of money for Louie's bribe
Used newspapers and racing forms (Annabelle, Louie)
Nurse's hat
Dress
White stockings
Shoes
Giant tongue depressor (Nurse)
Enema bag (Nurse)
Face wax foundation (Victor)
Wig for beast
Black pants for beast (baggy & primitive)
Black shirt for beast (baggy & primitive)
Hospital johnnies (Nurse)
Neck bolts (Nurse)
Burlap for beast shoes and coat
Fingerless gloves (Bag people)
Texas dirt for beast face
Fake long nails for beast

Baby picture of beast with initials "VS" on back
Note pad (Reporter)
Camera w/flash (Reporter)
Non-working gun (Detective)
Detective badge
Blood
Baggies with twists
Eye patch (Doctor)
Cotton balls (Frances)
Wig for Frances
Make-up for Frances
Eyelashes for Frances
Nails for Frances
Stockings for Frances
Boobs for Frances
Stretcher, sheet
Sign for entranceway
Clipboard (Doctor)
Cardboard box (Bag people)
Pillows
Donor cards
Mystery clue pads
Pencils
Resolution forms
Limerick
Lipstick for mirror clue
Chain, long, big links (Beast)
Straw
Bowl of water
Black cork for bag people
Dog collar for Beast
Hand-out music for sing-a-longs
Stick for Doctor
Watch on chain or crystal for hypnosis
Tissues for Doctor's blood pack

Empty cans for bag people
Styrofoam food container (Annabelle)
Coloring book page rhyme
Bribe money
Knife rig with blood for Louie
Face powder for beast
.16 Gun for Resolution (starter)